Manual

MW01206363

Content

The arrival of death always generates many doubts, because every deceased always wants to keep wandering, if you wonder what you can do or not when you die, you can solve each of these concerns, because the belief of the connection between the world of the living and the dead can be your reality when you lose your life.

Furthermore, there is no reason to believe that life stops when you lose your vital signs, but that from the afterlife you can attain the power and will to continue interacting, so as a dead person you may also be able to influence the living, and even see other dead people carrying out these powers.

How to know that you have passed away

The sensations at death are a key to understand the transition that your body is making, especially when losing vital signs progressively, about these peak moments there are different testimonies, either by people who revive from the beyond or by spiritualists who manage to communicate with the dead.

The study of experiences related to death, each time throws more progress and empathy can get to be close to that cold that arises, but you must take into account that not everyone lives the same episodes to have close contact with death, but after analyzing different stories, it is possible to form a general pattern.

The state of unconsciousness is the first phase you encounter when death arrives, which is always seen as a light that begins to emerge, like a totally pure wake, through an authentic glow that seems like being in a divine place, completely associated with heaven, this is the most common thing that is commented.

Death as a phenomenon is part of a sensation, especially before and during the arrest of the heart, and when the brain stops functioning, it is experienced as a consciousness that can last at least a few minutes, even by patients who are resuscitated.

But in the same way, many dead people claim that they feel nothing, that is to say, the experience is to enter precisely in a "nothingness", this can be common in accidents and sudden events, because it is as if immediately the body shuts down, as if taking a nap.

In turn, entering the world of the dead is described as waking up from a long lapse of time, it also arises as a mental gap because it is like a nap where you do not dream anything and only time has passed, thus experiencing the arrival of "nothingness", so it is believed that there is nothing similar to heaven.

As you become aware of being dead, the first thing you look for is to remember, but the previous moments are totally confusing, until you start tying ideas directly to the accident as a second and return to the current sensation where the absence of life haunts you, to enter a phase of intense pain.

Regardless of the type of beliefs, death is the same for everyone, at least the initial sensations, especially because there are many cases where the mind continued to be active, so it is interpreted as a kind of dream, because what is believed is that the brain continues to function as part of the experience associated with the dead.

- **The mental aspect of dying**

The mythical bright light that emerges at the end of the tunnel is an experience typical of these episodes, this is typical of what people experience when dying as part of the strange signs that arise when being on the verge of death, where you finally feel how the spirit is detached from the body and levitates progressively.

In the same way the famous bright light is presented to reach a point of total serenity, the difference between what one or another person lives, is based on the functions of the brain that stop working, and according to the type of death this changes, being an aspect ratified in a scientific way.

This kind of phenomena are originated by the mind, especially by the expectations of entering the beyond, so it is key to feel the tranquility of surrendering to death, from that attitude you can relax and not be fooled by what is happening, because then you can fall into the confusion of not knowing if you are alive or dead.

The mind's own reactions to a traumatic event that will provoke death can make you resist being dead, or try to over-understand what is happening, that is, when the mind seeks to understand what is happening, it makes the transition painful, since the perceptions are out of the ordinary.

The analysis of people who are on the verge of death is that they remain in a total alert because they feel danger, but this is also part of a biological reaction, so it can change for each person, that is why the typical emotions are the following:

1. **Euphoria and serenity**

There is no doubt that one of the most characteristic sensations of death is to develop different phases of consciousness, due to the response of making denial emerge, especially because one does not wish to cease to exist, which is why it becomes a real suffering.

Otherwise serenity helps you to project directly onto the sensation of levitating over your own body to transcend into death, all of which can arise artificially as a combination of perception and awareness of what is happening at death.

This sign of seeing the pure light, has much to do with an episode of euphoria, for that personal impulse to accept death and want to cross to the beyond, this is happening as the blood circulation is descending, the same happens with the oxygen level, for these situations is born the feeling of euphoria and serenity.

Chemically, this has to do with the brain's release of a hormone called noradrenaline, which causes positive emotions that can lead to hallucinations and other experiences that are part of one's personal vision of death.

All this is considered together, to issue a psychological result, in turn each experience can be influenced according to the type of feeling that results from being near death, this can be happiness, love, depression or other that goes through your mind, this happens because death is something unusual that has not been experienced before.

Once the brain stops working, is when different events are presented, these have no explanation because human perception has stopped working, so it feels much more real, and is a glimpse prior to death, that reflex is important to consider.

2. **The personal debate**

What awakens the sensations at death is the personal questioning about considering if you are dead, but the real question is if you are alive, to get an answer starts the questioning about the body, mind and behavior, to perceive some sensation that what you live is real or you are in the afterlife.

Therefore, when the answer is established on not feeling anything, as if the brain had rotted, as if there is nothing left inside you, that immediately produces a direct call to want to go completely to the beyond, the more you question yourself, the more answers you find that indicate that you are dead.

These thoughts in turn can be the ones that lead to death, while denial is another common sign that most present, this completely challenges intuition because you doubt that you exist, this is one of the deepest beliefs that you can live.

But the answer arises through the response of identity that each person has, so that the soul or that way of thinking that lives inside can transcend to another plane, that is to say the presence of the "I", moves to another plane, this is difficult to point out, because in this process you must face the collection of memories and you can lose some of them.

Possibly any decision or thought you wish to return to, will be too late because if you find out it is because you may already be dead, without being sure that when you wake up in the afterlife you will be the same person, much less have memories about that absence that is occurring.

- **What happens to you when you are dead**

The consciousness that arises from being dead manifests itself through a series of signs that each deceased person passes through, such as the following:

1. Ineffability. It is an experience that is presented as a refractor on the words, the lived and the language is transformed into something opaque.
2. A feeling of calmness, peace, and freedom from pain. It appears as a state of fullness that appears abruptly, with practically no memory of the previous state.

3. Awareness of being dead. You begin to hear with a different volume those around you, especially start talking about your death, this may vary by the sound of a whistling or buzzing.

4. Out-of-body experiences. The scene through which the death occurred is visualized, this can clarify many details about how the death happened or cause more doubts and pain.

5. Dark scenes. Once dead, the emptiness begins, like an enclosure, this is similar to going through a tunnel, especially because it is a narrow passage to reach the light, to find a climate of love and total acceptance.

6. Perception of being in a supernatural place. The place of death is described as a space that dazzles, you find colors and all kinds of extraordinary charms.

7. Encounters with other deceased persons. Encounters with other deceased is a common occurrence, especially as you begin to recognize family and friends, looking healthy.

8. Vision of an individual of light. The inner light begins to penetrate the place, and you feel inspired by it.

9. Retrospection in the form of a panoramic view. The past actions begin to reflect, to carry out a reflection on

everything that happens, it is like a much deeper empathy about everything lived and without making judgments.

10. Prognosis, Now as the deceased you can begin to see the fragments of your life ahead.

11. Belief of living in an eternal frontier. You believe or feel that a wall arises in the form of fog, with the deep fear that when you cross it you will not be able to return.

12. Conscious return to the world of the living. It is abrupt but some thoughts can travel directly to the world of the living to interact with the living.

Most of the consequences of being dead, have much to do with the loss of fear of death, but you begin to enjoy the power of it, because it makes it easier to see with a more generous view to human incidents, this is directly associated with empathy, especially when you live the death of a close relative.

What is most recommended and beneficial to perform better in the afterlife is meditation, because it helps to fulfill different objectives such as searching for a loved one who is dead, and after concentrating on your being, you can reach a high level of ecstasy about the nature of these events.

Advantages of being deceased

Death generates a lot of doubts or thoughts, but it is a situation that should be kept in mind, especially because it can generate important advantages that help to minimize this event, to gain another kind of vision, this is valuable to accept it as an everyday thing that everyone goes through.

Thinking about what happens after death should be a daily exercise, especially because it has many points of view, because if you are afraid of aging, when you die you stop this biological process, on the other hand, there is the advantage of the passage of time, because during death everything begins and ends on the same day.

In the same way, when you are dead all kinds of worries are put aside, since you do not face any kind of debts, that is to say, you are no longer stressed by such routine matters, and you do not suffer any kind of love sickness, doubts, or social commitments of any kind.

On the other hand, when you die you should not face physical pain of any kind, even your state of mind becomes free, since your last breath of life, takes away all these issues, that is to say, the complications end, this is a relief when you do not want to continue living for all these reasons, in that way the struggle ends completely.

The validity of death, has its positive aspect from these benefits, especially in cases of diseases or vital insufficiencies, so since you breathe you find yourself with these feelings, and it is common to practice medical suicide to end the suffering, so the reins of life go beyond death.

When having in mind the idea of death, you must consider that being ready or accepting the withdrawal from daily life, depends on the type of connection that exists at the level of body and soul, so that this feeling can be subjected to contrast, this is a priority when life deprives you of happiness, and fills you with burdens due to hopelessness or illnesses.

To have a life without life, is not a healthy subject for any reason, this must be submitted to the conscience so that the existence acquires value, without following a boring line, for the same reason the struggle and the transition towards death can be understood as a wisdom itself, to nourish you on the concept of life.

The duality between life and death is a blessed part of the consciousness, which can create a whole series of conflicts, since it must deal with a high level of uncertainty, so the most appropriate thing to do is to open up and allow the body to express itself until the end of existence arrives.

The first thing you should think about is the idea of living under the idea that you are going to die, and this should not diminish your vitality or that it is worth continuing. This point is something that very few people think about, but it should be assumed even from an early age, since assuming the end of existence can make you value life.

An ideology of this level can make you believe that by deciding you can think about what happens if you hold back and then something happens to you, so that you can follow a goal that generates satisfaction, this happens by going through and living year after year, to produce yourself, work, and strive to improve each time.

With each activity performed, you have the opportunity to dedicate time, with the freedom granted by the closeness to mortality, and this adds meaning to what you do, being a prior motive of consciousness to act and fight on a daily basis, so that the moments of vitality become completely worthwhile.

As far as your life goes, you can live under that level of adrenaline, that way morality also passes or descends to be in the background, but death above all should not be seen as a challenge in which you should go against, because getting to the end can be visualized as something difficult, it is not possible to stop thinking, above all.

- **Stopping thinking diminishes vitality**

Every human being, spends most of the time complaining, instead of taking advantage of every moment of life, when all these problems disappear at death, so the main thing you should fight and adapt with is life itself, so any question that goes through your mind has a reason to be and thinking is part of vitality.

Instead of spending your whole life subtracting, going through a complex coexistence, but it is part of the naturalness of the human condition, to deal day by day with the duality with the reality that you live and the final destination such as death, all this is combined, so the journey for many is a stage that can be overcome without suffering.

But it is inevitable that some people suffer after the acceptance of death, that is why in the afterlife expressions can be presented as a relief to stop any suffering, that means in a clear way that you can not look in a previous way neither the sun nor death.

Therefore, the best thing to do is to follow the paths of life, where you are the master of what happens, even about the sensation that you are going to find or wish to express when you die, without falling into the need to reach the limit of wishing death, because it would be to stop looking at what each day has in store for you from now on.

All this in sum recommends to think that dying brings advantages, because it ends many personal questions that do not let some people live fully, this is the end of the burden that dwells behind life, it is a way for suffering to end and it is possible to rest.

- **The other side of death; its benefits**

The perception of death as a sadness, pain, emptiness, always forgets to think of joy, when there is a positive point of view, as it is the rest of a lot of burdens, also from the biological aspect is an act that contributes to the continuity of the species, is a form of survival to consider.

Every element of the human body at some point dies, this is part of apoptosis, being a process that is directly associated with pain, but without death there would be no evolution, beyond that may arise unscheduled deaths due to the state of the organs, in the same way has benefits.

- **Forget about banal problems**

The cessation of life, is directly associated with stopping stress with issues such as stopping eating or going shopping for it, plus the bill coverage is released, at the same time that you will not have to work more, ie death is directly associated with an infinite time with your soul, so it is a more reflective stage.

The scope of death should not be assumed as something harmful, that is, when it occurs there are more aspects to consider to avoid the agony, but you can take advantage of that kind of state, so the basic thing is to value everything lived, both the good and the bad, without making judgments about your existence.

In death what makes the difference is the detachment of the physical body, so you will not even need to go to the bathroom, for this reason the occupation changes completely, because the daily life goes to the background, all the physiological aspect is changed by a more supernatural world, where you should not even take a shower.

That is why death is a freedom, a direct step towards meeting the memories, the deceased known and unknown, all this is merging to form or design the afterlife, having the possibility of living with the world of the living, so it is a spiritual responsibility that you must assume.

Rules of the world of the dead

The world of the dead develops from obvious limitations, especially when interacting with the world of the living, because the dead follow a line of behavior through which the absence of vitality must be respected, since when they lose vital signs and die, it is impossible to behave naturally and do the same.

The first thing that a dead person must deal with is the loss of fear, to assume his condition, and leave behind the materialistic vision because all that loses value in every way, because the physical spirit disappears with the arrival of death, then it is possible to advance to the world of the living without inflicting harm or fear towards others.

The control between two dualities, is what allows to guarantee that the dead can not move as if nothing, and above all that their role in life has complete cessation, so only through calls after a strong faith and ability, invoked from the world of the living, is that they can manifest, without acting as normal as they would like.

The reaction of the dead can not be reflected in reality, as an apparition as presential without obstacles, but may be related to close relatives, particular objects that you used frequently in life, which can be frightening, but it is a power the force to be or remain, as well as others to have another moment with the deceased.

It can be very serious and traumatic to encounter a spirit, but when there is unfinished business this is a common event, but at first the dead do not understand their strength, which is also limited to unlink the duality of the world, avoiding any kind of chaos and that the development of life is not interrupted.

It is impressive how the dead gain a totally timeless power of action, but for this the factor they must overcome is to have the perspective that they are no longer part of the world of the living, they will not be able to intervene directly with what happens for any reason, in the long run they only possess a reflective nature to ask for their own.

However, from the world of the dead a relationship can be created with the other deceased, where uncertainty dwells in some cases, and in others a deep conviction, many rules begin to apply for those who did wrong in life and are subjected to infinite punishments for their behavior in the world of the living.

The display of reality, always has many effects for the deceased, especially because it must be associated with the idea that he cannot speak, and above all that his memory may be being despised in the world of the living, therefore death implies a burial, an end and in theory the transit between both realities is very limited.

While it is true that phenomena provoked by the dead can occur, they have more to do with some break of a norm, by resisting to be part of this world or this new reality, therefore they can be subjected to a restoration in the world of the dead where they have no freedoms of any kind.

In the same way, the dead are always linked to an edge of ferocity and perversity, especially because when they cross the abyss, either by incantations, invocations or religions, they may appear to develop a charming ability, when in reality they seek to disturb others in order to generate problems.

The disintegration of souls completely is part of the belief of hell, but it is the greatest conviction that exists for souls to stop disturbing the real plane of the living, knowing beforehand that they can develop appearances that will only instill fear, and this completely alters reality and can challenge people's mentality.

The rules always seek to circumvent that fear that exists about the dead, because in the end what they want is not to be forgotten and the veneration of their deeds, since it is their only connection to the real world, but the reason for this has to do with the souls that become evil, to the point that the living have desires to protect themselves from it.

- **Rules of both worlds followed by the dead**

From the world of the living there is a great attraction for the dead, this occurs from the practice of cults, ancient beliefs, and any time or form in which humans would like to make an astral journey to meet the dead, and this acquires value because each person is a living unit.

Every living person at some point wishes to be reunited with the disappearance of the body of life, because once it decomposes there is a transition to another plane or other activities that are strongly regulated, because once each soul receives the light, it loses the decision to emerge in the plane of the living.

The dead have powers, but the control of the mind, heart and body is assumed by the supernatural aspect of dying, when trying to do this also with the living, arises what is commonly called possessed, and then that entity happens to be expelled from the beyond, because it is issuing orders in the world of the living and this is forbidden.

On the other hand, the dead are able to transmit the power to help heal the dead, that is to say, the energy of the shamans, for example, being close to the afterlife, uses the will of many dead people who have positive intentions, that is why there is so much talk about the good spirits and the ability they possess to restore strength to a patient.

The migration rituals that usually break the border between the world of the living and the world of the dead have been developed for more than seventy-nine thousand years, all thanks to the use that exists on the modalities of the soul, which is able to use the experience that exists beyond life.

The soul has always been baptized as the origin of life, but at the same time when the person dies, it still has strong ties with the world of the living for everything experienced, all this should be managed mostly is towards nature, this if it is allowed by the world of the dead.

The power and evolution that sprouts behind the stones, plants and animals, arises precisely because of death, this is an achievement that is part of the actions of the dead, that is, all that translates into the formation of rules that allow life to follow its natural course, from consciousness, reason and desires at the same time.

- **Crossing into life during rites and celebrations**

Much is said about the origin of a date such as the day of the dead, since it is an honor that becomes an attraction for the dead, especially because it may be allowed to produce some settlement, appearance, and so on, but from the total security for the living.

In various religions of the world, the feast of the dead is celebrated as a direct entrance, it is also a traditional epicenter, where a transition takes place, mostly to celebrate the passage from one year to another, but it can also function as part of the opening to the other world.

Each ritual has the form of a party, and the dead do not have the power to break with it, but there is a passage through which the dead walk with the living, and these in turn consider that this day can help to calm the deceased, it is a bit of peace that allow them to continue to meet their limitations.

- **Offering to the deceased**

In different cultures the offering of food to the deceased is practiced, and this facilitates their entrance to the earthly world, because their main instruction is not to enter without this type of call, which must have enough devotion for it to become a reality or at least for something to happen.

This kind of traditions is very useful for the dead who have left in traumatic causes, especially if they have not been buried, so they can achieve some peace for their well being, so they can assume their role in the world of the dead without infringing on the fulfillment of their place in the world.

Therefore the offerings can be useful for the journey to the afterlife can serve as a guide, at least works as an encouragement to be at peace, overcome the fact of being dead and follow the rules, not to affect the world of the living, nor to resist or cause harm, so the living maintain this behavior to achieve their liking.

The satisfaction of the dead is a reliable measure that can be followed, because it improves or alleviates the coexistence with the world they are currently living in. From this point of view, different names or classifications are added for the dead, according to their behavior in the world of the living.

Their appearance as human beings is not complete now, since they are souls without bodies, and according to their behavior in daily life they can be admired, feared or venerated, all this already depends on human subjectivity, which very little considers the coexistence of the dead, because life is an art that those who are still alive enjoy.

- **The dead cannot develop languages**

However, the communication emitted by the dead may be an interpretation of reality carried out by the living, or the whims of science itself, but the truth is that the dead do not have a language as such, they can perform signals or actions with objects mostly, but not express words.

According to life experience, some expressions of the dead, can be taken into account as a displacement of reality, because it has more to do with a private thought and that causes it to move away from the objective facts, this is a reflection to consider both the living and the dead.

That is, what each side or participant must recognize, is that what they express or interpret, does not necessarily fit with reality, because there is an incompatibility now that they are dead, they are not even part of the same world, so it depends too much on people with another degree of culture or religion, they can interpret some occurrence.

The attempts of a dead person, do not have any result in the world of the living, and only some fraction can be discovered, when there is a story that is analyzed by believers and people fully prepared for this means, so it is believed that the soul of the dead is the founder of theology or these studies.

The dialogue between the living and the dead is not as it is believed, actually if the living maintain a constant prayer with the dead, paranormal eventualities may arise, but not necessarily from that soul, nor through a natural or understandable way, besides the initiation and culmination for this to occur are the holidays.

Unless they are the dead in mourning, which are real, but neither transmit vitality nor reflection, they are only attached to the life that was displaced from them, previously for someone to talk to a dead person, even on a holiday, they needed to wear a garment or even blood of the dead, to create some kind of connection.

A connection must be intense, because death represents an experience of that same level, and it is ideal for each soul to be led, instead of avoiding rest, this happens mostly when they are wounded, or have an ailment that does not allow them to reach a state of spirit.

The deceased who wishes to remain united to the physical soul that has died, without a body, breaks his freedom and naturalness that awaits him in the world of the dead, this has sometimes been associated with the presence of a guardian something, but it is mostly about beings that are degraded and begin to be satanic and fictitious.

The punishment of not detaching from the physical body is a profound impediment to being a soul, because it is an incomplete deceased, until the separation is not carried out, they cannot be assumed as complete entities, and from the interiority of the living very little can be perceived.

They only possess opportunity when the very mind of the living unfolds its imagination, for they draw a sense of time upon themselves, and this is attractive to eternity, but when the dead follow every rule they may be regarded as spirits, for they follow and live the life of the gods without deviation.

For this reason, the idea between the spiritual and the immortal is so familiar, because being part of the world of the dead, in a way guarantees the tranquility and immortality that many dream of, this happens when the dead begin to develop experiences with themselves and are dazzled by the world of the dead.

- **The only relationships that the dead can form**

The ties to be strengthened by the dead, have to do with an interrelation with the spheres, stars, animals, and all forms of magic that are part of the world, the same happens with religions and their sacraments, they may be different, but what they have in common is the interaction with the dead.

A dead person becomes an entity, that is why in different cultures they can receive praise, but what keeps them at a distance is that the fullness of the world is developed by vitality and they lack it, that is why they have their own status of being subjected to an eternal rest, but they can arise for something they lack or feel they are owed.

For this reason, various divinities, both human and supernatural, return or bring back the dead, because they cannot concur with reality, it would be going against everything, beyond the fact that the feast of the dead exists, because the reality is that they are no longer part of this world.

In some cultures the idea that man is immortal is affirmed, but this is real from the point of view of the preservation of its parts, because every living being possesses a soul that does not die, but belongs to its time as is eternity, and cannot be associated with material entities.

The power of the thought of the dead, is what can cause them to leave their time, but then they remain without a body, since they are erased to not having a soul, thanks to the fact that they no longer possess reasons to be in the world of the living, because without the body they cannot be alive for any reason.

This can be interpreted as complex, but it is also one of the reasons why both worlds are incommunicable, mainly because they possess distinct realities, there is no equivalence in either, since they are entities that can be classified by the world as non-existent, and they do not possess an ordinary language.

Through different cultural areas, it can be believed that there is a language available, but no native sector endorses this, and makes it impossible for there to be a greater connection about both realities, but some deep meditations or sacrifices can originate revelations by the degree of pilgrimage that is developed.

But to achieve that kind of results, it is indispensable to have a high sensitivity, as well as a symbolic imagination of another level, using the essence of life to bring forth the dead, this kind of story was happening in some cultures, and depended entirely on the human spirit.

Although any event is tinged as a lie, because of the debate of whether it is a moral or mystical fact, which is complicated to assume as an earthly reality, because understanding it would be impossible for most, but they leave a profound teaching, to this is alluded that the living flee or are scandalized by what their eyes do not perceive.

Activities in the world of the dead

Throughout the world, through different religions, the dead receive a high level of attention and belief, which becomes an activity itself, this often allows them to be released a little of the rules of the world of the dead, but above all that culturally there is no forgetfulness of what they were or meant.

The Day of the Dead has a high level of transcendence in the world, especially because it has been understood as a celebration of faith, and is recognized worldwide by the development it has in Mexico, also this current was gradually infused by Latin America, with the sole purpose of honoring the dead.

This kind of festivity has gained a pleasant space in places like Bolivia, Peru, Guatemala and many more, even in the United States there is a development of this kind of incidences, to strengthen above all the relationship with the dead, this is assumed as a cult to life to consider it and have a total respect to death.

The pride of planning activities related to death, is a position that every Mexican is happy to assume, since above the sadness that can be assumed in other parts of the world, this celebration can be linked to life, as it is a bridge of reunion with the deceased, since they have the possibility of returning to the world.

The way of living and developing activities with death, is an aspect that is transferred from generation to generation, so it is common to continue placing altars, and practitioners reflect a clear sense of being accompanied or at least feel close to the world of the dead.

- **The culture and activities of the dead**

After several countries the celebrations of the dead change completely, because it has been rewritten as a day for the saints, but the point is the same, since it is sought that those who have departed to the world of the dead can not be forgotten, so in places like India, ceremonies of all kinds are developed.

At the same time with the celebration of these days, practices arise such as drawings on the ground to simulate the opening of the world of the dead, having direct contact with animals, making offerings to the dead, placing lamps on the river so that they go sailing.

But the excellence of this tradition remains in the hands of Mexico, because it develops a vibrant atmosphere where many stories affirm the connection with the dead, this can be explained from the degree of energy that is dedicated on each street, achieving that with altars the spirits can descend to coexist with the world of the living.

Each of these acts are part of traditions, and even in the least thought of corners of the world are appearing, it is a way to honor what has been lived, so the celebration is gaining more and more followers, with exhibitions of altars, music, parades, and much more.

Little by little the day of the dead is spreading over different corners of the world, so events of all kinds are organized, even in Paris celebrations are held in October, because it is the recognition of a magical world, through the gestation of important altars to celebrate the dead.

• The celebration of the dead in the world

Worldwide any holiday dedicated to the dead, receives different names, because it is known as the day of the dead, Halloween, the saints, Samhain and others, it all depends on the country, because the celebration is acquiring different denominations, but always keep in common the consideration with the dead.

The tribute to the deceased takes place at night, commonly under the dates of October 31, or November 1 and 2, for you can know one by one, the most influential points in the world that dedicate a day to the dead, are the following:

1. Day of the Dead in Mexico

From Mexico the idolatry about Catrina is developed, in turn the day is named after the dead, from the pre-Columbian origins, and it takes several days of the calendar to esteem the dead, where the main God is Mictecacihuatl who is recognized as the lady of death, who is known as Catrina.

The figure of this goddess has been followed for more than 100 years, to the point of being an insignia of the entire country, the celebration acquires greater specialty after the celebrations of November 1 and 2, during those days most areas in Mexico are covered with altars of all kinds to honor the dead.

In the same way it is common that a variety of offerings are presented, in the town of Aguascalientes, for example, there is a festival dedicated to the skulls, where there are parades and events where the altars are exposed, without forgetting the literary contribution that is put to the test during those days.

Even the gastronomy is inclined to this kind of celebrations, because during these dates the popular pan de muertos is offered, which is created as a bread in the shape of skulls made by candy and can also include the name of a deceased person known, this is done as an offering.

2. The celebration of Halloween in the United States

In the United States this day is also being baptized as the night of witches, recognized as a pagan holiday, has been rooted by the immigrants, since they transfer their traditions both Celtic and Christian, being a mixture between European and American residents.

This festivity takes place on October 31, but under the dynamics in which children mostly and adults, dress up as any kind of horror characters, for this night parties are developed, where the proximity of a bonfire is included, and some visit the cemetery as well.

Children comply with the tradition of going from house to house to receive candy, within this development is that they pronounce the typical words of "trick or treat", this is represented on a large number of series and movies, all this has spread progressively and also pumpkins, spider webs, and bats are used as decorations.

This name of Halloween has been one of the most international in the world, but the tradition lies directly on the United States, secondly, and other countries such as Canada, Ireland or United Kingdom, to launch a day where the most that is eaten are candy and caramel apples.

3. Samhain in Ireland

This kind of celebration is classified as pagan, with a strongly associated Celtic origin, thus it has become one of the most

popular celebrations in Europe, having repercussions and following Christianity, in fact, previously this celebration was
linked to the Celtic New Year.

These celebrations begin on October 31, everything started
from the dark period, because it was the end of the harvest,
so they kept their provisions for these days, understanding
that mythology indicates that the night of the dead, have the
opportunity to reach the world of the living to meet with relatives.

But in the midst of this return to life, there are also spirits that
are not entirely good, so practices were performed to ward
off evil spirits, usually food was used to expose it outdoors,
also for this the bonfires are lit, which also have the power
that the dead can take the souls.

In the same way, every assistant wore a mask so that the
dead could be confused, this was also introduced in some
sectors of the United States by the influence of the Irish who
were living in that country, that is why on Halloween there are
measures of this type, such as bonfires.

During that night a typical cake is prepared, it is called as
Barm Brack, where a ring is hidden and also a penny, when
cutting it if you get first to the ring, it means that you are close

to concrete some marriage and the second is associated with economic prosperity.

4. All Saints' Day in Spain

From November 1st onwards, the Day of the Saints is celebrated in Spain, this is recognized as a Christian holiday where a tribute is invoked for the deceased who are in the presence of God, in the middle of this day it is usual for people to go and visit the cemetery to make offerings of flowers and candles to the relatives.

On the other hand, masses are also held and some churches expose their relics, besides, instead of pumpkins, chestnuts or some other kind of nuts are used, in the case of sweets, what are made are the fritters of saints, each city can add other versions according to their local traditions.

In cases such as Catalonia, on the night of October 31, there is a festival based on the Castañeda, where most people begin to consume this nut, which can also be combined with the intake of panellets being a representative sweet of the region, while in Andalusia it is a day recognized as Tosantos.

On the other hand, in Cadiz the markets of the Virgen del Rosario or Central are developed, so that an entire carnival comes to life, where chickens, fish, pigs and rabbits receive a disguise, the change also occurs on fruits and vegetables since on these are applied caricatures on the characters of terror or the most striking of the present time.

In areas such as the Canary Islands, an atmosphere of joy is added to the night, because the party is carried out with music and various performances, on the contrary, in Soria is configured in a day to pay tribute to Gustavo Adolfo Becquer and the Monte de las Animas, where at nightfall the city is endowed with art.

In Alcalá de Henares there is full confidence in the theater, that is why we present plays related to the dead, because at the European level we seek to involve society with these ancient concepts of death.

5. Day of the Dead in Guatemala

From Guatemala the day of the dead is known as the giant barrels, as it is a continuity of the feast of All Saints, to take this opportunity to form altars, so you can remember and keep in mind the deceased, in the same way there is a tradition of visiting the cemeteries.

After the visit to the deceased, they can leave flowers, arrange the tombstones, and carry out a prayer for their loved ones, but the most fervent ritual is the aforementioned giant barrels, which is originally from Santiago Sacatepéquez, is celebrated during November 1 and 2.

This kind of celebration is based on throwing barrels into the air, on a hill that is close to the cemetery, for this purpose designs are made by groups of friends and neighbors, this is done for months, to have a good time in which the barrel is kept in the air.

6. **Saints' Day in the Philippines**

In the Philippines, this date is called the day of the saints, to develop a religious festivity, during every moment there is a high level of joy, because everyone wants to honor their deceased, and the epicenter of the festival takes place in the cemetery, this happens on the morning of December 1.

Most families gather at the cemetery to spend the day with the tombstones, as a kind of reunion with the deceased, for which a whole banquet is held with large amounts of food and drink, so that the party goes on all day long without limits.

The most typical thing is that there are even karaokes and card games, then when the day is over, the Filipinos dedicate themselves to completely clean the tombstones, that way everything remains as it was, the only thing that remains is the tribute that can be made by means of the flowers.

7. **Day of the Dead in Brazil**

The name that is applied in Brazil, is the "día dos finados", recognized even as a national holiday, to commemorate the dead, this was consecrated in Brazil thanks to the contact with Portuguese immigrants, so the celebration has great similarities with the way it is developed in Spain.

The day occurs on November 2, so that Brazilians can go to the cemeteries, thus staying close to the deceased, the difference is that this is practiced in different cities of the country, instead of being only in one, but all seek to deploy prayers on the tombstones of their loved ones.

What is sought is that the souls can have peace and can not leave purgatory, for this the tombstones are cleaned, candles are placed and some wreaths of flowers is usual to place personal items of the deceased, such as hats, t-shirts, photos and many other details.

8. **Ancestor's Day in Cambodia**

Since Cambodia this kind of celebrations are carried out with the description of Pchum Ben, being the same as the day of the dead in other parts of the world, but with the philosophy that on that day the door to hell is opened, and it is believed that the souls that have not been reincarnated, cannot come back to life and avoid mixing in the world of the living.

For the deceased to follow the path of good, this kind of celebration is held, but for this the relatives offer food, and at nightfall the pagodas that are part of the country, are full of believers who attend to provide an offering, also during the night the monks start all kinds of chanting.

The reconduction of souls is the main objective of all these actions, so that the lost souls do not generate chaos, and before it becomes daylight the Cambodians sleep, and then the city is in full silence waiting for the deceased to take the offerings made.

During this kind of festivity, there are no other similar celebrations in other parts of the world, this means that it is a unique event, because it follows the Khmer calendar, and the holidays start from September to October, that is why behind each celebration there is a certain particularity or fervor.

In different parts of the world, the remembrance for the dead is latent, especially in exotic places with roots and preeminence of ancient culture, so these days are worth gold for both worlds to concentrate positive energies, these organizations are very positive for the conduct of the dead.

Laws of the deceased

The deceased have natural and supernatural laws, in the case of the natural laws they are based on the understanding that life has concluded to leave their body, while the supernatural laws have more to do with the stimulus of the world of the living to find the right path towards that transition that causes death.

A natural law for the living, is to take care of the memory of the dead, this is even interpreted as a ritual that remains after the arrival of death, as this idea of remembrance is greater or collective, the greater the results will be, because the hope that the deceased will not be forgotten is still alive.

The presence of a deceased person remains in force, through that collection of memories that they leave with their existence, to this is added the symbolic act of accompanying their departure with flowers, as a form of tribute to honor what they have been in life, that is why many cultures practice it from love, without considering the relevance it has for the world of the dead.

The evidence of this law for the deceased, has much to do with the residues of the traditions of Rome, where even the flowers are used as a means of decoration, but the concept was deeper than that, this was demonstrated by biblical evidence, where even mostly pink carnations were used.

The preference of this type of flowers, is due to the fact that they are the first ones that emerged on earth, under the mythical story that arose after the tears of sadness of the Virgin Mary, at the same time the rosemary acquires the name of this divinity as it is; "Rose of Mary", and therefore has great value for the admiration of the dead.

In turn, the great literary contributions such as Hamlet also recognize the value of flowers on funerals or before the deceased, because rosemary is used to keep alive the memory, and in turn is a great way to get to pray, and not lose the image of what was, so the flowers also represent a good unification of memory.

- **Other symbolic measures for remembering the deceased**

Often talking or conversing about the deceased also helps, because it becomes an exchange of memories about what the deceased lived or meant, this at the same time for the world of the living, leaves a great margin of comfort, because it is like getting hope and renewal of what remains to be lived.

The association of a conversation and flowers with resurrection has a lot to do with that natural symbolism of death, this is in turn a renewal of encouragement for you to acquire a better picture of what is happening, rather than relying solely on sadness, so it is an important change.

At the same time above the biblical evidence, the Neolithic arises, where it is confirmed that the flowers and the memory of the deceased is a key requirement, on this inhabit facts dating before Jesus, because it has been found pollen on the funeral homes that are part of the Neolithic period, as they covered with this to the deceased.

The bodies of the deceased and the fulfillment of the laws, are mostly speculative, but they are traditions that should not be broken, because the use of flowers for example is a good representation of the man in the future, that is to say of a life, and visually releases any kind of sadness.

On the other hand, the aspect of the smell of flowers, contributes to the bodies to have a better abandonment of the world of the living, that is why later in the burials began to apply strong flavorings, but the need continues to dwell behind the floral offerings, to be a strong custom.

Likewise, for some time the influence of the size, shape, and color of flowers to pay tribute to a deceased person has been evaluated, because this can count for a smooth crossing, and in the past hearses had to be carried by horses as a clear representation of the passage to death.

As a deceased person is no longer mentioned or given importance in the world of the living, by law he or she gradually disappears, so as a defense or as a way of holding on, they may carry out scares to keep his or her presence alive in the world, at least from the spiritual point of view.

This explains in a clear way the reason why some deceased people wander around and appear before their relatives, the same happens when they want to claim their objects and interests, for this reason it is important that they are dismissed from the world with these elements, in that way the spiritual peace is much closer.

- **Faith to dedicate on the deceased**

A law of great preeminence over the deceased, is the contribution of their interests, therefore the most preferred items are added in life, above the population and customs are varied, these inclinations are still held in society, because it is important to cover the subject of flowers.

In some religions, instead of flowers, gifts are placed, because this is part of the rules of the afterlife, these can even be represented by fruits as a symbol of life, this in turn can bring happiness to the environment, and the color white is a symbol of respect and admiration for the deceased.

In the same way, in the face of difficulties when some person from the world of the living keeps talking to the deceased, he/she will continue to acquire validity or power, this is important so that they can appear and generate some kind of sensation over the living, such as a cold from nowhere or moving objects.

The scent that arises as that of flowers, also strengthens the sense of peace that a deceased acquires, because it can be transferred directly to that environment or sense of liberation that is presented on death, for this reason it is treated or interpreted as a much more harmonious way in all aspects.

Following these laws maintains a control and a clear coexistence between two worlds or two realities, therefore the behavior carried out on one or the other, is capable of altering this process, this implies that maintaining certain symbolic aspects is a necessity in all aspects for the development of death to be full.

- **Love over grief**

Within the natural law, it is vital to assume the departure of that person on the earthly plane, thus knowing that he/she will no longer be in the world of the living, the next thing to do is to follow the rules of the beyond by adopting a better attitude so that it is not an absolute loss, but an ascent, this mentally and spiritually is liberating for both parties.

Memories are the only thing left on earth by the deceased, but for this the crossing of the mourning becomes necessary for the deceased to rest, because concentrating on the past, only demands sad and nostalgic energy, but there is no turning back and the deceased is in the place where he/she belongs.

The threat of remembering with sadness, leaves nothing good for the world of the dead, therefore the key steps are to let go of grief, so that the deceased does not have that call to the afterlife, on the other hand, there is the rule of avoiding excessive suffering to justify loving the deceased more, because that only prevents him from leaving.

What you should stay with is all the positive acts that the deceased has emitted, and then concentrate on doing or acting as that person would want, in that way you are fulfilling his will on earth, by following his point of view, in the same way you should start to build a link between love and death.

But the most important thing is not to forget the deceased for any reason, so that his spirit does not wander, but is able to take its place without clinging, this is key so that there is no excessive suffering on either side, causing the process of death can flow naturally.

- **Farewells are an innate act**

A key to death is that the farewell to the life of the deceased can be produced or gestated, this should not be altered, or at least it should be compensated by paying the true respect they deserve, formal acts are highly appreciated to close the life cycle of the deceased, that way they can really pass on to a better life.

The mourning and the correct farewell, removes the feeling of anguish that arises over the deceased, therefore it is an important point in all senses, it is the best way to control the impotence of being dead, this is useful and has greater power when it receives sincere accompaniment.

Karma and the harmony of the spirit

Death demands and develops directly on karma, so any kind of materialism is put aside, to focus on the human actions that really make the difference between life and death, so that the fear of dying fades little by little and you can move on to help others.

The contribution to others is then released to themselves, because the meaning of life cannot be defined solely on personal goals, since that selfish vision is like walking dead in life, because at some point you will feel that nothing makes sense and that leaves behind vitality.

But a good intention cannot be developed from the intent of wanting to save others, because that only feeds your ego, but when you act only for a welfare, you can manifest a kind of liberation, because beyond oneself, what you need to manifest is the desire to help.

Acts of this type have nothing to do with death, but with the real development of life, otherwise there is a fear of death, not only from one's own death, but also from the death of others, which in turn is a total attachment to life, when it does not belong to anyone.

But this at the same time is a consequence of religions, because most of them try to find an explanation for death, when it should not be seen as a negative event, but as a clear warning that time is not something to be lost, and that every instant is a gift.

The instant is based on a precession of death, thus death can be acquired as a stimulus to live, where the existence of karma is established as an important trace, especially because it emerges in the form of consciousness and this is manifested at the moment when the spirit is detached from the body and takes its stains with it.

But the spirit is not carried away by the past karma, that is why it is known as a liberating moment, where any condition of the past is left aside, that is why death is called the game of freedom, because at death the person does not adhere to anything.

- **The effects of karma on death**

The experience of the past is formed on karma, and as it can be dissolved, each deceased person gains space over his life because everything is unknotted, the abolition of the past karma happens as a tax payment, it has consequences in the afterlife, but it passes to the background completely.

But as it is known, there is positive karma and negative karma, where the control and wisdom of each decision is assumed as positive karma, but when negative karma is present, death itself anchors the spirit to remain in contact with the stains of karma, both its own and that of society.

Purification is a supervening necessity of death, to work through a work of personal transformation, therefore in life you cannot deny karma for any reason, as it would be dangerous, especially because it is impossible to escape this law, so the line that comes into force is that of the consequences of everything you do.

Even a thought has its own consequences, that is why karma has fruits that you must learn about, so that in life itself you can be attentive and aware of what you do, to coincide to a much more beneficial outcome, over and above your own surroundings.

Instead of feeding or contributing to suffering, it is crucial to avoid irresponsibility, because ignoring karma does not free anyone from guilt, therefore karma awareness is a study to take respective action on karma, this is what cures any kind of feeling or sense of guilt.

- **The law of cause and effect**

Suffering is always desired to be avoided, but everything starts from what karma means, because it is mostly confused as a punishment when in fact it does not represent this concept, but what it really represents is the way in which each person is responsible for what he/she is capable of sowing and what causes beyond life.

The understanding behind karma starts from the initial cycle of life, therefore it goes hand in hand with birth, life and death, this is a circle that has no beginning, much less end, but death is established as a kind of temporal closure, this is what constitutes an important place on reincarnation.

Karma itself represents an action, it has much to do with the type of seed that is planted after the world, and depending on the intention or quality will be the result that can be harvested, so the words can be sown to germinate, this is described as the consequences that are presented.

The karmic law is part of the universe, where everything that is sent is subsequently received, this sooner or later may return, this is an individual result that is generated behind everything you do, that is why suffering occurs according to the way you acted.

- **Death as a teaching in the face of karma**

The understanding of death is strongly associated with karma, especially because it is a relationship with the actions developed in life, but it is not a concrete reality, far from it, everything has more to do with a spiritual and reflective character, which in turn implies an understanding of existence.

Ultimately, karma is not the one that estimates what will happen after death, but everything depends on how you have behaved in life, where death is imposed as the liberation of all those negative causes, until bequeathing a perpetual existence in the afterlife.

Death has a starting point to be considered, and it always generates a kind of change in the way of acting, because it is a way to know oneself, to know how to go through and assume the death, from the inside one can find an adequate way to live as well as to die.

It is useless to create false visions about death, because it is something you do not know, and only at a deep level can you have an idea of it, especially when some situations arise that put you on the edge of everything, no matter how much you contemplate the end of existence, it is inevitable and represents a way of transformation.

There are different guidelines that can help you cleanse and get rid of karma, because the responsibility behind every act also extends to regulating the level of karma you can develop. That way you can not only get on track for death, but start living better in all aspects.

Today's existence is part of past actions, so the kind of decisions you make have a great influence on the results of karma that may arise, because in reality the consequences of actions always arise, and this is taken into account by the forces that are above man.

The acts on the environment, even the simplest, are adding up to an interrelationship called karma, this defines all the movement that is behind a previous result, even the emotions are capable of generating something, so in the world every little aspect counts.

The representation of karma arises in different ways, either from the emotional, to the mental, this in turn can be transferred to the physical plane, so what you should think about is to improve your life to assume any bad decision and thus the response by karma can change.

Therefore, it is essential to take these aspects into account:

1. Everything you do, you get.

2. Each being is the creator of each of the life experiences that he or she generates, so after a correct visualization of the world, you will be able to make the right decision.

3. Gratitude is a form of evolution, because nothing is one's own, but existence is the owner of it.

4. What happens is part of the consequences of one's actions, thoughts and also emotions, these can be from the past or the present.

5. Everything that happens is interconnected, therefore any act has an effect on others, so the most equitable law of life is to treat others as you wish to be treated.

6. The only thing that has a forever is change, since change itself is part of growth.

7. The advancement of every person is carried out step by step, with a direct view towards the goal without losing track of what is happening now.

8. Abundance goes hand in hand with generosity, so what you give you can receive.

9. The past is a fleeting wake, as it passes, the future resists, therefore there is no place for regrets or punishments, but to maintain concentration on a focus.

10. By assuming the same paths, it is impossible to change the reality we are living.

11. Every kind of evolution has its time, these periods deserve to be respected, and the movements must be exhausted progressively.

12. To achieve any proposition, it is key to dedicate soul, body, and mind as well, that way you reach a maximum.

The safest thing that can be experienced prior to death is to receive all that you have harvested, by understanding these points you can look at existence with different eyes, everything is based on advances and cycles that are characteristic of life, so that each action, thought or emotion has its own weight.

• **Death after the contrast of good karma and bad karma**

The teachings from an early age about acting well, have a lot to do in the long run with death, because when thinking about karma this event is strongly associated with a type of judgment, to determine what you deserve to receive at death, but these realities have many nuances or points in between.

What exists after death may have to do with karma, especially the acceptance or rejection of what you are, all this is manifested at the end of existence, because it is a retribution on your life, and at the same time once you die begins a phase of purification.

The self-examination after death, follows an optic of love in all aspects, because any action can be fixed, but the simple fact of losing life is an event that has no return, life itself moves to another type of existence, this is even recognized as a reunion with what you are or have been and with another one.

From karma, death does not represent a tragedy, unless you are escaping from that encounter with your soul, it is an appearance that begins every day when you ask yourself the reasons for which to live, this is the preparation to fulfill what you are, that is why there is no other judge than your own actions and conscience.

Death can be understood as an ultimate end, to identify personal and deepest realizations, to truly feel a state of bliss, that is why leaving life must always follow a line of gratitude to have happiness and not lose sight of the true beauty behind life.

Living is open to those who can be in communion with death, especially because behind this is the personal identity, for this you can begin to meditate and leave aside the forever, since it is a temporary stay, so the most appropriate is to live every situation with a high dose of faith.

What really is forever will be the fullness found at death, and at the same time there are great advantages such as noticing how little or how banal the value of things in the world of the living is, in comparison to the freedom that is described in detachment and death, as an act that everything that begins, must end.

The true change of death is that there is no betrayal or deception, but a general beauty as a form of greatness that challenges any science, therefore during existence every temporary project must be an absolute goal because the exact end cannot be measured, but by means of a horizon of the end.

Any concern rests in its entirety at the end of life, but what concerns the spiritual life, is where it is really lost, because facing the world of the living you can no longer participate, but you have an infinity to gain once you have passed away, the most important thing is that there is a degree of consciousness about the acts.

Suffering after death, beyond being associated with the causes of death, also has to do with the type of role you had on earth, because it depends on it to reach that fullness and joy, so it is said that after karma there are punishments, but they are teachings or points of view.

In the same way, from the world of the living it is possible to support the deceased from prayer, this is done in favor of the dead, to honor their memory, but also so that they have that stimulus of strength to fight against the suffrage, that vision of praying can be interpreted as a request or payment for the transition of the deceased.

From a reflective view it is possible to clean the defects, but above all to identify oneself with them, to start from the recognition of dishonest acts, to focus more on doing something without gaining merit, that is a measure from now, until always, because everything that is done is to give pleasure to existence.

The arrival of death, is a moment with all that behavior you have developed, and being detached from your actions is what is known as hell, because in the end you have the choice to recognize these aspects, otherwise from the very being there is a self-exclusion.

Death under negative karma, it is like following an end forever, that is why there is the existence between good or bad karma at death, where sorrow is the impediment for man to reach the happiness for which he exists, so you should not refuse to believe and become what you have done.

Ascension to heaven and tips for getting out of limbo

From the experiences of Jesus and his resurrection, the promise of the ascension to heaven was extended, in the case of Jesus it took place in a real way because he returned bodily from death, but his disciples and other followers continued to wait for him, this made the ascension to heaven a very important manifestation.

In the first place, human action has limits, this is recognized as a success in having fulfilled its mission on earth, that glory is described by the time spent on earth, which at death is imposed as a reception, that is, each person must be pleased with it, as an honor.

The stay with other people is a gift itself, this is part of the evidence that places Jesus above as a God inherent in man, so the look of any is installed on the after death, thinking of some kind of reincarnation or even bodily return.

But really the manifestation of ascension is a way of remembering that the final goal of every being is heaven, that is to say the end of a performance after death, therefore it is vital to leave traces on every environment, besides the path is traced by each one from their positive or negative actions.

Deliverance from death, is the strongest motive for which a deep belief about Jesus is created, as it is a feat on the subject of resurrection, and everyone expects that separation from earthly life, to move on to an ascension, to work on one's beliefs, with the goal of returning.

The announcement of the second coming of the spirit, is destined for the end of time, this is a phrase issued by Jesus precisely on the mount of ascension or also known as the mount of olives, so this idea has a high level of celebration, and even in the Jewish level has great influence.

An ascension not only has to do with a physical action, but it is a spiritual position, this is called as the purification that allows the rest of the souls, also this allows you to listen and be guided by a supreme God, so it has a significant point in everyone's life.

In itself the ascension represents the closing of a circle, in this case of human existence, but above that still remains alive and remains present for believers, but during this process there are many doubts, where the only certainty is that the goal is based on the fact that heaven remains the goal or destiny of every man.

This process complies with a process strongly associated with reincarnation, to be raised from death, for this various prayers are issued, especially in which the gospels continue to predict the ascension that will occur as an honor, because Jesus resurrected has saved humanity.

- **Preparing a place in heaven**

The place in heaven is always proper to each individual, because according to the biblical evidence, when Jesus ascended, he initiated a kingdom that has no end, but it is always a position that stages heaven and earth, where humanity is part of the word and of life itself.

Behind the grace of believers, there is the promise of no longer living under a dismay, much less remaining in what has happened at death, that is to say overcoming limbo, on this also depends that the human mission has been shared and overcome with goodness in every way.

The conjunction between life and death does not mean that there is a path of pain, but it demands a more believing attitude, and above all in constant prayer so that humanity can wait for the end of time or of its existence with a promise of tomorrow.

The pilgrimage of a God on earth is what has given the world more hope, because the Lord, having given instructions, was sent to heaven, since then he has been followed, awaited and above all looked at differently than what lies behind death.

The ascent arises after Jesus demonstrated that he was alive, because really a soul does not die, beyond that this reflection refers widely to a bodily aspect by the type of divinity that these acts reach, but what is clear is that many pursue the arrival at the kingdom to have a rest without torture.

The times and moments are never recognized by man, but the designs of life are part of the manifestation of the holy spirit, so every time men take a step towards the future or towards death, it is impossible to take your eyes off the sky as the destination of it.

The ascent is made in the midst of the acclamations, with trumpets and other acts that God generates, because he is the king of the world and as such is able to rule over every nation, that divine glory, is able to grant or issue wisdom and relief to come to know man completely.

The illumination that exists over the eyes and hearts of men, is a way of transmitting hope, especially because the wealth is granted by the saints who emit a greatness and a power that a God works above all, therefore according to what you believe a beyond is manifested.

Everything that constitutes man goes with him, with the hope of going to heaven as it has happened with Jesus, therefore this is a religious precept that everyone worships above any doubt, thanks to the fact that Jesus possesses full power over heaven and earth, and this is a great consideration.

- **Everything behind limbo and how to get out of limbo**

In the midst of death, limbo is presented as a timeless state, where the souls of people who have died and are believers are found, given that their death occurred prior to the resurrection, also in limbo are found people who have not been baptized or who have died at an early age.

Similarly, limbo leaves many types of interpretations, such as the inclusion of people who did not infringe any personal sin, but were not baptized and do not comply with the Christian doctrine, this follows the line of original sin and valued strictly to a single form of baptism.

This is strongly disputed after the resurrection, because it is not believed that God could exclude someone from paradise, dealing with children who have died without receiving baptism, especially since divinity advises that God frees the innocent from any torment that may arise in hell.

The requirement of baptism has to do with carrying the original sin with them, and they may not receive punishments, but they may have prohibitions at the moment of having access to paradise, that is why the idea of limbo has taken value over Catholicism and became a strong doctrine.

But the Catholic Church does not follow this type of position, because it is not part of their dogma or faith, instead purgatory is much more recognized, this is because limbo is dedicated to people who have a great burden of sins and seek absolute mercy at death, but through the Bible this place is not recognized.

The mixture between purgatory and limbo is that one is more accepted than the other, since purgatory is known as a way to enter heaven at death, this state does not classify as hell, far from it, but it is a phase where different sufferings begin to manifest.

All this constitutes the transformation of the soul to achieve cleansing, and to leave aside the sins, in that way it will be able to enter heaven, all this forms a way of purification in which the soul of the dead is guided, this can be achieved through the Eucharist or religious indulgence.

On the other hand, when it comes to limbo, it has much to do with an eternal stay, where there may not be any suffering, but the souls of the dead are destined to wander or be under this phase for eternity, without the possibility of going to heaven or hell.

The existence of limbo is rejected, but purgatory is nevertheless approved, because it does have biblical evidence and is narrated with many details about paradise, purgatory and also heaven, for which prayers are made to God, so that he can have mercy on the souls of the dead who are in these phases.

- **Reconciliation with limbo**

The existence of limbo and purgatory is discussed about different religions, everything can be inconsistent, but the most appropriate is to comply with baptism in order not to fall into any state of limbo at the moment of death, since these measures help the soul to be guided, from the petition and the way in which love is exercised.

The entrance towards a state of good fortune is produced from the consciousness of positive acts, besides you must avoid living under a superficial vision, because all this will be paid on the final judgment, this is known as the worst hours in the life of every man, especially after life.

This concept is transmitted from different religions, to overcome the wall that leads the deceased to the afterlife, also this facilitates that the souls can not escape from hell, and those who do not have access remain in that state.

The border zone on death and the climb to heaven, is sought to exclude or leave aside to rescue the end of the souls, as long as there is a difference between good and evil, to overcome the idea of limbo, from the actions themselves, this is the path that is infused on stories of souls in pain.

Instead of waiting for that destiny of children without baptism, the first thing is to comply with this type of belief requirement, beyond that there is no formal confirmation, these measures are a great option to have a destiny or a less painful transition, for this you must save yourself and be happy after death.

In order to go to the destination of the deceased as soon as possible, it is necessary to receive help from prayers, so that the world of the living can function as a kind of guide, which is doubly appreciated because the deceased will be able to receive blessings, that is why it is traditional to carry out masses and prayers.

The admiration and gratitude that is behind the prayers for the deceased, is part of the good feelings and emotions that help every soul, with so many frequent deaths after different causes, it is best to establish prayers at a general level for the deceased in the world, so that they find peace.

There is no doubt that the soul of children must be cared for above all else, that is why baptism is a key step, to turn to the faith, since the twentieth century the idea of limbo is part of existence and seeks to avoid, above all, especially to get rid of original sin, first of all, since St. Thomas Aquinas this concept is configured.

- **The place and the escape from limbo**

Limbo is shaped as a place for children, they can be totally happy as long as they can overcome the condemnation of being in that state, it is believed that the voices of salvation arise during baptism, therefore it is an act that can reconcile in favor with the salvation of their souls.

The rituals of blessing have much to do with finding a more certain path with less torture after death, the measure of baptism should be used as a clarity on the soul, and the church itself invites each person to attend its celebrations to receive divine mercy.

Praying for the salvation of the soul is a tradition that opens step by step, in that way one can avoid the possibility of being in limbo, but the final verdict of what happens at death has much to do with faith, this is studied in depth by theology, and reinforces the importance of baptism.

The existence of limbo cannot be completely denied, because it appears in many stories, and when it is entered it is like a disappeared soul, in the same way it can have other ways that save the transcendence of the soul and it is related to the Eucharist, but from baptism it can at least be supposed to have a type of salvation.

But the blessing of baptism, and other acts, does not arise only after death, and likewise limbo has a waiting time, so it is not a definitive state, much less eternal when interceding for your soul, but in past centuries this was completely doubted, but the truth is that salvation exists.

All this means that after death hope can be kept alive, especially for those little souls who for years were so marked, but the answer is after the death of Christ, because he has done it for all without exception, because all men can be saved.

The important thing is that people can approach their beliefs, that way you can count on God's mercy, this is greater than any kind of sin, this is affirmed by any scripture, where every biblical quote recommends that Christ died for all and is the part of the divine reality.

Holding and following the Holy Spirit, is part of being associated with the Easter events, where the most that can be highlighted is the solidarity of men, to continue believing in the resurrection, since every person is enlivened by Christ, regardless of the abundance of sin, righteousness will always reign.

Even though all have sinned, one cannot be deprived of the glory of God, because they are justified through the redemption that Christ had, that is why it is part of his will that no soul is lost, as long as human solidarity with Christ can be highlighted as a priority of life.

Made in United States
Troutdale, OR
09/25/2024

23120148R00040